Preliminary Notes

Nigerian English
In his novel, *No Longer at Ease*, Chinua Achebe gives examples of the many different kinds of English spoken in Nigeria. However, in this retold version, the re-writer has shown some differences in the way people speak and has used language which the reader will understand. See Glossary no 31, page 16.

Historical
Nigeria became an independent country on 1st October, 1960. This story is set in Eastern Nigeria in the 1950s. At the time, the British ruled Nigeria, but they were getting ready to leave the country. Nigerians were given higher positions in the Civil Service.

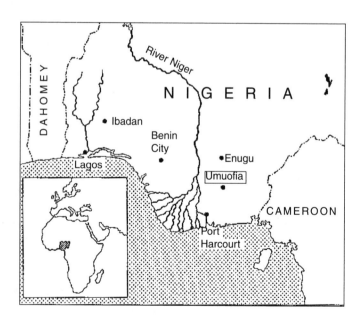

Prologue

In the Courtroom

Everyone in Lagos was talking about the trial[1]. On the last day of the trial, the courtroom was full.

The young man on trial was Obi Okonkwo, a Senior Civil Servant[2]. Obi Okonkwo was accused of taking a bribe[3]. After Okonkwo was found guilty, the Judge spoke to him.

'I cannot understand why you took this bribe,' said the Judge. 'You are an educated young man. You are a young man of great promise[4]. I cannot understand why you did this.'

When Obi heard these words – a young man of great promise – tears suddenly came into his eyes. The tears began to run down his cheeks. He quickly took out a handkerchief and wiped his face. He did not want anyone to see that he was crying.

Obi had lost everything. He had lost his mother. She was dead. And he had lost Clara – the woman he loved. She had left him, for ever. Obi Okonkwo had nothing more to lose.

But when Obi heard these words – a man of great promise – he started to cry.

At the Officials' Club

There were many Europeans at the Officials' Club[5] that evening. Mr Green was there. Mr Green was Obi Okonkwo's boss[6] in the Civil Service. Mr Green had been in Nigeria for many years.

The man from the British Council was there too. He had not been in Nigeria very long. He and Mr Green were having a drink together.

'I can't understand why he took the bribe,' said the man from the British Council.

'I can,' said Mr Green in a loud voice. 'I know why he took the bribe. The truth is that all Africans take bribes.'

'You are a young man of great promise. I cannot
understand why you did this.'

The other people at the bar stopped talking and listened to what Mr Green was saying.

'We have given the Africans an English education,' went on Mr Green. 'But what have they done with it? Nothing at all. They don't understand that it's wrong to take bribes. They have always taken bribes. The young man in court today took a bribe. Why not? He was doing what every other African official does. Why can't you understand that?'

At a Meeting of the UPU

That same evening, in another part of Lagos, the members of the Umuofia Progressive Union[7] – the UPU – were holding a meeting.

The members of the UPU had all been born in Umuofia. Umuofia is a village in Eastern Nigeria, about four hundred miles from Lagos. Umuofia is not a big village. But the Umuofians are very proud of their village.

Every member of the UPU paid part of his salary[8] to a fund. This money would be used to send young Umuofians to be educated in England. Obi Okonkwo was the first Umuofian to be sent by the Union to study in England.

But Obi Okonkwo had been found guilty of taking a bribe. And the members of the UPU were meeting to discuss[9] what they should do. One member said that they had helped Obi Okonkwo enough.

'We paid eight hundred pounds to send him to study in England. Was he thankful? No, he was not.

'We sent him to England to study law[10], so that he could become a lawyer. If he had become a lawyer, he could have helped us in our court cases. But what did he do? He changed his course. He studied English Literature instead. And what good is English Literature to us?

'Then he got involved with an unsuitable woman[11]. He has given us enough trouble. Why should we give him any more help?'

The other members knew that all this was true, but Obi Okonkwo was an Umuofian. He was the first Umuofian who had gone to study *in England. The members of the UPU had to help him as much as they could.*

The President of the UPU did not ask why Obi had taken a bribe. He did not understand why Obi had taken such a small bribe.

'It is shameful[12] for a man who has a good job in the Civil Service to go to prison for twenty pounds,' the President said angrily. 'Twenty pounds – what can you buy with twenty pounds? Why did he take a bribe of only twenty pounds? If you are going to eat a worm, you should make sure it is big and fat.'

―――――

The Judge, the man from the British Council, the President of the UPU – none of them understood why Obi Okonkwo had taken the bribe. Mr Green said he knew why. But was Mr Green right?

When we have read the story of Obi Okonkwo, perhaps we will understand why.

1

Obi Leaves Umuofia

At the age of twelve, Obi Okonkwo passed his Standard Six examinations with distinction[13] in every subject. He won a scholarship[14] to one of the best secondary schools in Eastern Nigeria. After five years, he passed the Cambridge School Certificate, again with distinction in every subject.

Obi Okonkwo was the first student the UPU sent to England. The UPU gave Obi eight hundred pounds so that he could go to study in England. The eight hundred pounds was a loan[15] which Obi promised to pay back later. He would have to repay it when he had finished his studies in England and had a good job back in Nigeria.

When Obi was getting ready to leave for England, there was great excitement in Umuofia. A few days before he left, his parents invited everyone to their house.

Huge pots of rice and stew were placed on a large table in front of the guests. Jugs of palm wine[16] were placed beside the pots of rice and stew. It was a great feast. It was the best feast that the Umuofians had seen in many, many years.

After the guests had finished eating, the minister[17], Mr Ikedi, gave a long speech. As Mr Ikedi finished speaking, he turned to Obi.

'You are leaving us,' said Mr Ikedi. 'You are going to England to study and to find knowledge. But remember that you will meet many temptations[18] in the white man's country.'

'I have heard sad stories about some young men from our country, who went to England to study,' Mr Ikedi went on. 'These young men did not work hard at their studies. They went dancing with women who were not suitable. Some of them married white women.'

Everyone shook their heads. That was a terrible thing to do.

'So Obi,' said Mr Ikedi, 'you must not go dancing with women who are not suitable. We are sending you to England to study. You can enjoy life later, when you have completed your studies.'

The meeting ended with a hymn and a prayer. As they were leaving, the guests said goodbye to Obi. They all shook hands with him. As they shook hands, they each gave Obi a small present. A shilling to buy notebooks. A penny to buy a pencil. They were all very small presents. But they were very large presents for poor people who worked hard on their small farms, day after day, year after year.

2

Obi's First Visit to Lagos

Obi stayed in Lagos for a few days before getting on the plane that took him to England. When he was a small boy in Umuofia, Obi had heard stories about Lagos.

'There is no night in Lagos,' a visitor from the big city told the villagers. 'At night, the electric light shines like the sun.'

Obi never forgot these stories about the bright lights of Lagos. When he arrived in Lagos, these were the first things he saw.

Obi was met at the bus station by Joseph Okeke, a friend from Umuofia. Joseph was a clerk[19] in the Nigerian Civil Service. He was much older than Obi, but they had been at junior school together.

That first night, Joseph and Obi sat talking until three o'clock in the morning. Joseph told Obi about the cinema and the dance-halls and about political meetings.

'You must learn to dance,' Joseph told Obi. 'You won't get a girlfriend if you can't dance.'

Joseph's talk about girlfriends excited Obi. He wanted to know more about this strange and sinful[20] new world. Joseph talked and talked. But finally, they both fell asleep.

The next day, Joseph had a visitor – a young woman. The young woman was wearing a red and yellow dress which fitted close over her body. Her lips and her long fingernails were painted bright red.

The woman did not look real. She looked like a painted doll. Obi remembered Mr Ikedi's words.

Obi saw that Joseph wanted to be alone with his girlfriend. So Obi went out for a walk alone.

3

Clara Okeke

Obi was away in England for almost four years. To Obi, the time seemed much longer. The long English winters made him feel cold and miserable. He often thought of his home country – Nigeria. His stay in England made him feel proud[21] to be a Nigerian.

Now it was time for Obi to return home. He was not going back by plane. He was going back on a small boat which carried only twelve passengers.

Obi put his case in his cabin[22] and went to join the other passengers in the lounge. There was Clara Okeke! She was sitting in the lounge talking to a young Englishman.

Obi had met Clara once before. He had met her at a dance

for Nigerian students in London. Clara Okeke had come with a Nigerian student who knew Obi.

Obi had thought Clara looked very beautiful. He had watched her dancing with other men. Finally, he was able to dance with her. But Obi was not a good dancer. After the dance ended, Clara had gone off to join her friends.

Now Obi and Clara were going back to Nigeria on the same boat. Once again, Obi saw how beautiful she was.

Obi sat down beside Clara and the Englishman.

'I think we have met before,' Obi said to Clara.

Clara looked surprised and a little angry.

'At a dance for Nigerian students in London,' Obi went on.

Clara was not interested. She turned away from Obi and went on talking to the young Englishman.

Obi went back to his cabin and read a book. Sometimes he went on deck[23] to look at the sea. This was the first time he had travelled by sea. He had heard other Nigerians talk about seasickness. But so far, the sea was calm[24] and he was enjoying the journey.

At breakfast, Obi sat down at a large table with ten other passengers. Clara was sitting at the same table, but Obi did not look at her or try to speak to her. Obi thought she was being cold and unfriendly to him. So he decided to be cold and unfriendly to her.

On that first morning, all the passengers were hungry and ate a large breakfast. But during the day, the weather changed. The boat began to roll about on the rough sea. Obi went to the dining-room for supper, but he could not eat anything.

He went back to his cabin and lay down on the bed. Suddenly there was a knock on the door of his cabin. He opened the door and it was Clara.

'I saw that you did not look very well at supper,' she said, speaking in Ibo[25]. 'So I've brought you some tablets[26]. Take two before you go to bed. They will help you to get to sleep.'

Obi began to thank her, but she said in English, 'I'm a nurse. I've brought enough tablets for all the passengers. Goodnight. You'll feel better in the morning.'

Obi did not sleep that night. He thought all the time about Clara. She had been friendly at first. She had spoken to him in Ibo – their own language. But then she had spoken in English. When she spoke in English, she was not friendly.

Did she want to be friends with him or not? Obi could not make up his mind[27].

Obi got up early the next morning. He felt better. The deck had been washed and it was wet. He had to walk carefully. He stood at the side of the boat and looked out over the sea. Then he heard footsteps. He looked round. It was Clara.

'Good morning,' he said, with a friendly smile on his face.

'Good morning,' she replied and started to walk away.

'Thank you for the tablets,' he said in Ibo.

'Did they make you feel better?' she asked in English.

'Yes, very much.'

'I'm glad,' she said and walked on.

Obi turned again to look out over the sea. Then he heard someone falling on the deck. It was a young Englishman. It was the Englishman Clara had been talking to in the lounge.

Obi helped the Englishman to stand up. And from that moment, they became friends. The Englishman's name was John Macmillan. They played table tennis together and they drank together in the bar. They called each other John and Obi.

'How old are you, Obi?' John asked one evening, as they were sitting in the bar.

'Twenty-five,' replied Obi. 'And you?'

'The same as you,' said John 'I'm twenty-five too. How old do you think Miss Okeke is?'

'I think she's about twenty-three,' replied Obi.

'She's very beautiful,' said John. 'Don't you agree?'

'Yes,' replied Obi. 'Very beautiful.'

13

One evening, the boat stopped at Funchal – a port on the islands of the Madeiras. After supper, Obi and John decided to go for a walk through the small town. John invited Clara to go with them.

'It's very pretty,' said Clara, as they walked through the narrow streets and the little gardens and the green parks.

They arrived back at the boat a few hours later. The other passengers had not come back. There was no one on the deck of the boat.

'I'm going to my cabin,' Macmillan told them. 'I've got an important letter to write. See you in the morning.'

He went to his cabin. Obi and Clara were left alone.

Obi and Clara looked at each other for a moment. Suddenly, without a word, Obi took her in his arms. He kissed her again and again.

'Leave me,' she whispered.

'I love you,' Obi whispered to her.

She stood silently for a moment. He held her in his arms. Then she pulled herself away.

'You don't love me,' she said. 'You'll forget it in the morning.'

She suddenly pulled Obi towards her and kissed him. Then she pushed him away.

'There's someone coming,' she said.

She ran back along the deck and down to her cabin.

Obi took her in his arms.

4

Bribery and Corruption

Obi's interest in Nigeria had become stronger when he was in England. He often went to meetings of the Nigerian Students' Union in London. He once gave a talk on the reasons for corruption[28] in Nigeria.

Obi said that there was corruption everywhere. Young men and old men were corrupt. But the reason for corruption was the old Africans at the top of the Nigerian Civil Service. The old men must be replaced by young men – young men who had been educated at university. When these young men were given important positions, they would stop the corruption.

On his return to Nigeria, Obi soon found examples of bribery and corruption. When the boat arrived in Lagos, the first people to come onto the boat were the customs officers[29]. A young man came to Obi's cabin. He saw that Obi was bringing back a radiogram[30]. He told Obi that the duty on the radiogram was five pounds.

'Write a receipt for me,' Obi said to the young man.

The young man looked at Obi for a few seconds. Then he said: 'I can make it two pounds.'

'How?' asked Obi.

'I do it, but you no get government receipt[31].'

Obi became very angry. He said he would get a policeman. The young man ran from the cabin. Obi waited for another officer to come to his cabin. An officer came, after all the other passengers had gone. Obi was the last passenger to leave the boat.

Obi soon found other examples of corruption. The Umuofia Progressive Union held a big meeting to welcome Obi back to Nigeria. The Secretary of the Union made a long speech. He praised[32] the Umuofia Scholarship Scheme, which had made it possible for Obi to study in England.

Now that Obi was back in Nigeria, he would get a good job in the Civil Service. He would be able to help other Umuofians.

And, of course, Obi would repay the loan. The money would be used to send other Umuofians to study in England.

After the speeches, the President of the Union spoke to Obi about his future.

'Have you been given a job yet?'

'Not yet,' replied Obi. 'I'm going to an interview[33] on Monday.'

'Perhaps we should have a talk with the men on the Interview Board,' said the Secretary, who was standing beside the President.

'That will not be necessary,' said the President. 'Most of the men on the Board will be white men.'

'You think white man not take bribe?' said the Secretary. 'Come to our department. The white man take bribe more than black man nowadays.'

5

'Our Love Must Be a Secret'

After the kiss on the boat, Obi fell in love with Clara. As soon as she was back in Lagos, Clara was given a job as a nurse in a big hospital. She lived in a small flat.

Obi went to visit her. He asked her to marry him. She did not say no. But she would not let him buy her a ring[34].

'Wait until you get a job,' she said. 'Don't tell anybody about us,' she went on. 'Our love must be a secret.'

After the meeting of the UPU, Obi went with Joseph to a restaurant for a meal. While they were eating, a long black car stopped outside the restaurant. Obi could see into the back of the car. A handsome young man came into the restaurant. Everybody turned to look at him.

'That's the Hon Sam Okoli,' whispered Joseph.

The Honourable Sam Okoli was a well-known politician. He was over thirty, but he looked much younger. He was tall and handsome and smiled at everybody.

But Obi was not looking at the Honourable Sam Okoli. Obi was looking at the long black car. There was a woman sitting in the back seat. It was Clara.

Is that why she doesn't want to get married? he asked himself angrily.

Now I know why she doesn't want anyone to know about us, thought Obi. She's in love with this Honourable Gentleman – the Hon Sam Okoli.

6

The Interview

There was more talk about bribery at Obi's interview. At first, the interview went well for Obi. The Chairman of the Interview Board was a fat, friendly Englishman. He was interested in literature and poetry. He asked Obi what poems he had studied at university.

The two of them talked about poetry for a long time. The other members of the Board did not know anything about literature. They pretended[35] to listen carefully. But one member was asleep.

After some time, the Chairman turned to the other members. 'Have any of you any questions?'

They all said no, except the member who had been asleep. He woke up suddenly and spoke.

'Why do you want a job in the Civil Service?' he asked. 'So that you can take bribes?'

Obi was very angry.

'I don't know how to answer your question,' he said. 'If I wanted the job so I could take bribes, I would not tell the Board, would I? I don't think your question is very useful.'

'It's not for you to say which questions are useful,' said the Chairman, smiling. 'You will hear from us later.'

Joseph was not happy when Obi told him about the interview. Obi thought that he had given a good answer to the question about taking bribes. But Joseph did not agree.

'You must be respectful to your superiors[36],' Joseph told him. 'You have been to university and you have read books. But I am older and wiser. I tell you that it is important to respect your superiors.'

'Nonsense,' said Obi. 'It was a silly question.'

That evening, at supper, Obi asked Joseph about his girlfriends.

'You used to have lots of girlfriends,' said Obi. 'Where are all your girlfriends?'

'I'm going to get married,' replied Joseph. 'I haven't got any money to spend on girlfriends. I must save up to pay the bride-price[37]. I must save one hundred and thirty pounds. And I am only a clerk. On my salary, it is not easy to save money.'

'But there has been a new law passed about bride-price,' said Obi. 'The law says that no one must pay bride-price.'

'The law!' laughed Joseph. 'Everyone pays bride-price. It's

higher than before. You will get a good job in the Civil Service and you will have to pay more. When you want to marry, you will have to pay a bride-price of five hundred pounds!'

'I'm not paying five hundred pounds for a wife,' said Obi. 'I'm not even going to pay fifty.'

'Then you will never get married,' said Joseph, with a loud laugh.

7

On the Road to Umuofia

While he waited for the results of his interview, Obi went on a short visit to Umuofia, his home town. He travelled first class. First class meant that he sat on the front seat with the lorry driver and a young woman with her baby.

Two policemen stopped the lorry after they had travelled about forty miles from Lagos.

'Damn,' said the driver. 'What do they want?'

'Show me your papers,' said one policeman. The driver got out his papers from a box under the seat. The driver's mate[38] went to talk to the other policeman. As the driver's mate was going to give something to the second policeman, the policeman saw Obi looking at them.

'What do you want?' the policeman shouted angrily at the driver's mate. 'Go away! You want me take bribe?'

The first policeman found something wrong with the driver's papers. He took out a notebook and began to write. At last, the driver got back into the lorry and drove off.

About a quarter of a mile along the road, he stopped.

. . . *the policeman saw Obi looking at them.*

'Why you stare at policeman when my mate try to give him two shillings?' he asked Obi angrily.

'Because it's wrong to take bribes,' replied Obi.

'Why you book people put your nose into other people's business?' asked the driver. 'When I see you, I know you make me trouble. All you book people the same. Now I pay ten shillings, not two.

It was then that Obi understood why they had stopped. The driver's mate had run back to bribe the policeman.

'How much they take?' asked the driver when his mate returned.

'Ten shillings.'

'You see,' said the driver to Obi. 'You see what you do. Now I pay ten shillings, not two.'

The driver did not speak to Obi for the rest of the journey. The woman with the baby fell asleep.

Obi thought about Clara. He had asked her about her friendship with Sam Okoli.

'Are you in love with him?' Obi had asked her.

'Nonsense!' Clara had replied. 'Sam and I are old friends that's all.'

And Obi knew that she was speaking the truth. But she still wanted their love to be a secret. Obi could not understand why. Obi slowly fell asleep, still thinking about Clara.

Suddenly the lorry came to a stop. All the passengers woke up.

'What go wrong?' asked the passengers in the back of the lorry.

'I fall asleep,' said the driver.

The passengers in the back of the lorry laughed. They began to sing songs to keep the driver awake. He started the lorry again and drove off. But Obi did not sleep for the rest of the journey.

8

Back Home

At Umuofia, everyone was waiting on the road to welcome Obi. There were school bands and church bands playing music as he arrived. The whole village was having a feast. The old people were sitting in front of Mr Isaac Okonkwo's house.

The villagers were worried that it might rain. The villagers had asked Isaac Okonkwo to visit the rainmaker[39] and give him gifts. The rainmaker would make sure that it did not rain. But Isaac Okonkwo had refused.

'I am a Christian,' he told them. 'I do not believe in rainmakers. It will rain or it will not rain. God has already decided. Rainmakers cannot change God's decision.'

There were hundreds of people at Isaac Okonkwo's house. After the first four hundred handshakes, Obi was able to sit down in the big room with his father and his older relatives.

'The white man's country must be far, far away,' said one of the old men. Everybody knew it was far away, but they wanted Obi to tell them about it.

'When I was on the boat,' said Obi, 'there were many days when I saw no land at all. No land in front, behind, to the right and to the left. The sea was all around us for day after day.'

'Think of that,' said the old man. 'No land for day after day!'

'Isaac,' said another old man to Mr Okonkwo, 'you must bring us a kola nut[40]. We want to give thanks for this child's safe return.'

'This is a Christian house,' said Obi's father. 'Kola nut is eaten here. But we do not eat kola nut to please the spirits.'

'Who talked about pleasing the spirits?' said the old man. 'I want to give thanks for the child's safe return.'

He stood up angrily and left the room.

'This isn't a time for quarrelling[41],' said another old man. 'Here, I shall give you a kola nut.'

'Do not trouble yourself,' said Mr Okonkwo. 'I will give you a kola nut.'

Isaac Okonkwo went into an inner room and came back with three kola nuts. He put them in front of the oldest man in the room. The oldest man was not a Christian, but he knew how the Christians prayed. He said a prayer in which he spoke the name of Jesus and everybody was happy.

When all the visitors had gone, Obi's mother came and greeted him. She put her arms round his neck and held him. Tears came into Obi's eyes. He saw that she had become old and thin. Obi saw that she was a sick woman. And Obi saw that his father too, was not well. He was thin and weak. Obi saw that they did not have enough to eat.

Isaac Okonkwo had been a teacher in the church for thirty years. Now the church gave him two pounds a month. But most of the money was given back to the church. Mr and Mrs Okonkwo had eight children. Obi, his brother John and six daughters. The two youngest children were at church schools and Isaac had to pay their school fees. The youngest boy, John, was going to go to grammar school. They had to find the money for his school fees.

The money from the church had never been enough. They had grown vegetables and sold them in the market. And his mother had made soap and sold it. But now they were too old to work. And they were too poor to buy the food they needed. It was shameful.

After his father had said prayers, they all went to bed. Obi lay down but could not sleep. His father and mother needed help.

When I get a job, Obi thought to himself, I must send them some money every month.

But how much? Could he send them ten pounds a month? He had to pay back the loan from the UPU. He would have to pay them back twenty pounds every month. Would the Union let him pay the loan back later? He would ask them.

Obi stopped thinking about money and started to think of Clara. Why had Clara said that he must not tell his parents about her? He wanted to tell his mother. His mother would be pleased to hear that he was going to get married. She had once said that she would be ready to die after she had seen his first child.

Why did their love have to be secret? Why was he not allowed to tell anyone about her?

It began to rain. The rain fell down onto the iron roof. Obi had forgotten it could rain so heavily in November. He stretched out comfortably and slowly fell asleep.

9

'I Cannot Marry You'

Obi had done well at the interview. He got a letter from the Board telling him that he had been given a job. He was to be a Senior Civil Servant in the Scholarship Board. He was to be Board Secretary. His job was to look at applications for government scholarships to overseas universities.

When Obi arrived at the office of the Scholarship Board, he was taken to meet his boss, Mr Green. Mr Green did not get up from his chair and he did not shake hands with Obi.

'I hope you enjoy your work here,' Mr Green said to Obi. 'I'm sure you will find it enjoyable if you work hard and if you aren't a fool.'

Obi was sent to work for a few days in Mr Omo's office. Mr Omo had worked in the Civil Service for thirty years. Obi was sent to work in Mr Omo's office in order to learn about the job.

A few hours later, Mr Green came into Mr Omo's office. Mr Omo jumped to his feet as soon as Mr Green came in.

'Why hasn't the local leave file[42] been brought to me?' Mr Green asked.

'I thought . . .'

'You are not paid to think, Mr Omo. You are paid to do what you are told. Is that clear? Now send the file to me immediately.'

'Yes, sir.'

Obi decided that he did not like Mr Green or Mr Omo. Suddenly the telephone rang. Mr Omo picked it up as if it was going to bite him.

'It's for you,' he said to Obi. Obi took the telephone.

'Have you been given a letter to take to the car-dealers?' asked Mr Green.

'No, I haven't,' said Obi.

'You say sir to your senior officers, Mr Okonkwo,' said Mr Green and he put the phone down with a bang.

Obi was given a letter to take to the car-dealers. The letter said that Obi was a Senior Civil Servant. So he was going to be given a loan to buy a car.

Obi went to the car-dealer and showed him the letter. Obi was immediately given a new Morris Oxford.

Later that morning, Mr Omo asked Obi to come to his office to sign a paper.

'What's this for?' asked Obi.

'It's for your clothing allowance[43],' said Mr Omo. 'You think Government give you sixty pounds without getting your signature?'

The junior clerks in the office laughed at Mr Omo's joke.

'This is a wonderful day,' Obi told Clara on the phone. 'I've got sixty pounds in my pocket and I'm getting a new car at two o'clock. Let's go out to dinner.'

Obi paid a driver ten pounds a month to drive the Morris

Oxford. Later that day, he sat in the back of the car with Clara. The driver was taking them to a restaurant twelve miles outside Lagos. They were going there to have a special dinner.

But neither the drive, nor the dinner, was a great success. Clara was not happy. Obi tried to make her smile.

He told her about the government flat he had been given. The flat was in Ikoyi, an expensive part of Lagos. At one time, only Englishmen and their families lived there.

But the news about Obi's new flat did not interest Clara.

'What's the matter?' Obi asked.

'Nothing. I don't feel very happy. That's all. I will tell you about it later.'

'When?'

'After dinner.'

Neither of them ate very much. After the meal, Clara wanted to go and see a film. Obi said no. He wanted to find out why she was so unhappy. They went for a walk.

Obi tried to kiss Clara.

'I cannot marry you,' said Clara suddenly. And she burst out crying.

'I don't understand you,' said Obi. 'I really don't. Tell me, why can't you marry me?'

She did not reply. She put her arms round him and began to weep.

'What's the matter, Clara? Tell me.'

'I am an *osu*[44],' she said as the tears ran down her cheeks.

Suddenly she stopped crying and took a step back from him. Obi said nothing for a few seconds. He stood looking at her in silence.

'Now you see why we can't get married,' said Clara.

'Nonsense!' shouted Obi. He shouted the word loudly. He was trying to forget those few seconds – those few seconds when he had said nothing.

It was very late when Obi got back to Joseph's small flat. He opened the door quietly, but the noise woke Joseph up. Obi sat down in a chair and told Joseph what Clara had told him.

'So that's the reason,' said Joseph. 'That's why this beautiful girl has not been married until now. You are lucky to have found out.'

Joseph saw that Obi was not listening to him.

'I'm going to marry her,' Obi said.

'What!' Joseph sat up in bed.

'I'm going to marry her.'

'You are a fool,' said Joseph. 'Listen to me. Do you know what an *osu* is? But how can you know? Your long stay in England has made you forget.'

'Of course, I know. But I am going to marry the girl.'

Joseph did not say anything more. He turned over in his bed and was soon asleep.

Obi knew there would be many others, like Joseph, who would be against the marriage. But this was the twentieth century! It was unbelievable! It was shameful that people still believed in such a thing.

Many, many years ago, Clara's great-great-great-great grandfather had become the servant of a god. 'He had become an *osu*. His children and his children's children had all become *osu*. An ordinary person could never marry someone who was an *osu*.

'But I will marry Clara,' said Obi, as he lay down on the bed. 'No one – not even my mother can stop me.'

On the following day, Obi met Clara at half past two. He immediately told her that they were going to buy an engagement ring.

'But I haven't said that I will marry . . .'

'Don't argue,' said Obi. 'I'm moving into my new flat in Ikoyi tomorrow and we have a lot to do. I haven't got any pots or pans.'

They were driven in the Morris Oxford to Kingsway, the biggest shopping centre. They went into a jeweller's shop and bought a ring for twenty pounds. Obi was spending his clothing allowance very quickly.

Then Clara said that he must buy a Bible.

'Why a Bible?' asked Obi.

'You always give a Bible with an engagement ring. Don't you know that?'

When they had bought an expensive Bible, they went shopping for pots and pans and other things for Obi's flat. At first, Obi was interested in buying the things that were needed for the flat. But after an hour, he lost interest. Clara was never happy with anything. They went from one shop to another. But Clara always found a reason for not buying something. Obi followed her round like an obedient dog.

When Obi got back to Joseph's room, it was nearly eleven o'clock. But Joseph was not asleep. He was waiting for Obi to come back. Joseph wanted to talk to Obi about Clara.

'How is Clara?' Joseph began.

Obi did not want to talk about Clara immediately. He talked about the shopping and the drive in the car. Then he added: 'By the way, we are now engaged. I gave her a ring this afternoon.'

This news surprised Joseph and made him unhappy.

'Are you going to follow the custom[45] and ask your family to meet her family?'

'I don't know yet,' replied Obi. 'I will have to ask my father.'

'Your father will not agree to this marriage. I'm sure of that.'

'I will talk to my father,' replied Obi. 'He will agree. And my mother too.'

But Obi knew that his family would not agree to him marrying an *osu*.

If my mother agrees, he thought, everything will be all right.

'You don't know what you are doing,' said Joseph. 'If you marry an *osu*, your children and your children's children will become *osu*. One day in the future, anybody will be able to marry anybody. But that day has not come yet.'

'It's too late now,' said Obi. 'I have given her an engagement ring.'

'Our fathers did not marry with engagement rings,' said Joseph. 'It is not too late to stop the marriage. Remember, you are the first Umuofian to be educated in England. What will the poor men and women who gave you the money to go to England think of such a marriage? They will not be pleased.'

Obi was beginning to get angry. 'The money was given as a loan. I will pay back every penny.'

10

At the Meeting

The Umuofia Progressive Union held a meeting on the first Saturday of every month. The next meeting took place on 1st December 1956. Obi remembered that date, because it was important in his life. It was the day when things began to go wrong.

Joseph phoned Obi from his office.

'You have not forgotten the meeting?' he asked. 'It begins at half past four.'

'Of course not,' said Obi. 'I'll meet you at four o'clock.'

When he put the phone down, Joseph told the other clerks in his office: 'That was my good friend. He just back from overseas. BA Honours.'

'What department he do work in?' asked one of the clerks.

'Secretary to the Scholarship Board,' replied Joseph.

'He go make plenty money there,' said the clerk. 'Every student who want go England go see him at house.'

'He not be man like that,' said Joseph. 'Him gentleman. Him no take bribe.'

'That true?' asked the other. But he was sure that it was not true. All Civil Servants took bribes.

At a quarter past four, Obi arrived at Joseph's office in his new Morris Oxford. That was why Joseph was looking forward to this meeting. He was going to arrive with Obi in his new car. It was going to be a great day for the Umuofia Progressive Union when one of their sons arrived in a car.

Obi and Joseph's arrival in the car was a great success. All the members clapped their hands and cheered and danced when they saw the car arrive.

Obi was given a seat beside the President. He had to answer lots of questions about his job and about his car. At last, the meeting began.

They talked about the problem of Joshua Udo, a messenger in the Post Office. Joshua had lost his job because he had been sleeping at work. Now he wanted the UPU to lend him ten pounds to help him to get another job. Everyone knew why Joshua needed the money. It would be used to bribe someone to give him a job.

Before the members agreed to give him the loan, the President spoke to Joshua.

'You did not come four hundred miles from Umuofia to Lagos to sleep. You came here to work. If you don't want to work, you should go back to Umuofia.'

One of the members disagreed with the President.

'It is not work that brings us here to Lagos,' he said. 'It is money. Anyone who wants to work can stay at home. There is plenty of work in Umuofia. He can clear the land and dig the hard soil. He can work to the end of his days, but he will not get any money.'

Everyone agreed that they had come to Lagos for money and not for work.

31

Then Obi was asked to speak. He thanked them for the kind welcome they had given him on his return from England.

'And I will always remember,' said Obi, 'that it was you who made it possible for me to go to England. I wish to thank you all for the help you gave me.'

Obi began his speech in Ibo. Later he spoke sometimes in Ibo and sometimes in English. This pleased the members of the Union. They understood Obi when he spoke in Ibo. And they pretended that they understood him when he spoke in English.

At last, Obi spoke about the loan which the Union had given him.

'I have a small request[46] to make,' said Obi. 'As you know, it is not easy to live in a new place. It costs a lot of money.'

All the members laughed.

'My request is that you wait four months before I start to pay back the loan.'

'Your words are very good,' said the President when Obi finished his speech. 'I do not think anyone here will say no to your request. We will wait for four months. Are we all agreed?'

'Ya!' the members all shouted in reply.

'But before we finish,' went on the President. 'I want to speak to you like a father. You know book. I do not know book. But I have lived a long time and I am older than you. So I am not afraid to talk to you.'

Obi's heart began to beat quickly. What was the President going to say?

'Lagos is a bad place for a young man,' the President went on. 'You get a very good salary. You get more in one month than some of your brothers here get in one year. I have already said we will wait for four months before you start to pay off the loan. We can wait one year. But are we doing you any good?

'Your salary is more than enough for you. But it will not be enough if you get into bad ways. Remember, we have all come from Umuofia. We are here to help our town and our families. We must not drink because we see our neighbours drinking. We must not run after bad women because we see our neighbours running after bad women.

'You can ask why I am saying all this. I have heard that you have been seen with an unsuitable woman. I have heard that you are planning to marry this woman who is unsuitable . . .'

Obi jumped to his feet. He was shaking with anger.

'Please sit down, Mr Okonkwo,' said the President quietly.

But Obi did not sit down.

'You cannot speak about any woman like this,' he shouted. 'I am not going to listen to you. Forget about my request. I will start paying now. This minute.'

Obi moved towards the door. A number of people tried to stop him. 'Please sit down!' 'Don't leave!' Everyone was talking at the same time.

Obi pushed his way through the crowd and ran to his car. Many members ran after him asking him to come back.

'Drive off!' Obi shouted to the driver as soon as he got into the car.

Joseph pulled the car door, trying to open it.

'Obi, please! Please come back!' he shouted.

'Get out!' shouted Obi.

The car drove off. Half-way to Ikoyi, Obi told the driver to turn round and drive back to Lagos, to Clara's flat.

Obi pushed his way through the crowd and ran to his car.

11

Temptation

Obi began to like his job. He was given an office. Mr Green's attractive, English secretary was in the same office. Her name was Miss Tomlinson. Obi did not see Mr Omo and Mr Green very often. He saw Mr Green when he ran in to shout orders at him or Miss Tomlinson.

'He's a strange man,' Miss Tomlinson said once when Mr Green had gone out. 'But he's not a bad man.'

'Of course not,' replied Obi.

Obi agreed with Miss Tomlinson because he knew she might be a spy[47]. Secretaries were often put in the same office as an African to spy on them. They always pretended to be friendly. Obi knew that he had to be careful when he was speaking to Miss Tomlinson.

As the weeks passed, Obi began to like Miss Tomlinson. One day, Clara came to see Obi at the office. When Clara left, Miss Tomlinson praised her.

'Isn't she beautiful? Aren't you a lucky man? When are you going to get married?'

After that, Obi and Miss Tomlinson became friends. He was sure that she was not a spy.

One day, the telephone rang and Miss Tomlinson answered it.

'It's for you, Mr Okonkwo,' she said. 'There's a gentleman downstairs who wants to see you.'

Obi went downstairs. A man was waiting for him.

'Good morning,' said Obi. 'My name is Okonkwo.'

'My name is Mark. How do you do?'

They shook hands.

'I've come to talk to you about something, Mr Okonkwo,' said Mr Mark.

'Come up to my office. We can talk there.'

'Thank you very much.'

Mr Mark followed Obi upstairs.

Obi opened the door of his office. Mr Mark stepped in. He stopped suddenly when he saw Miss Tomlinson. But he smiled at her and said, 'Good morning.'

'Sit down Mr Mark,' said Obi. 'Now, tell me, how can I help you?'

Obi was very surprised when Mr Mark began to speak in Ibo.

'Is it all right if we speak in Ibo?' asked Mr Mark. 'I didn't know there was a European in the office with you.'

'If you wish to,' replied Obi.

'It's about my sister,' began Mr Mark. 'She has just passed her School Certificate with Grade One. She wants to apply for[48] a scholarship to study in England.'

Mr Mark spoke in Ibo. But there were some words he had to say in English. Words like "School Certificate" and "scholarship". Mr Mark spoke very quietly when he said these words.

'You have come for application forms?' asked Obi.

'No, no. I have got these. I have come to see you because you are Secretary of the Scholarship Board. We are both Ibos and I want to speak to you like a brother. You know what happens in our country. If you do not see people, you . . .'

'It is not necessary to see anyone,' said Obi. 'Send in the application forms and . . .'

'I wanted to see you at your house,' said Mr Mark. 'But I did not know where you lived.'

'I'm sorry, Mr Mark,' said Obi in English. 'But I can't help you.'

Mr Mark was surprised when Obi spoke in English.

'I'm sorry, Mr Okonkwo. Perhaps this is the wrong place to talk about . . .'

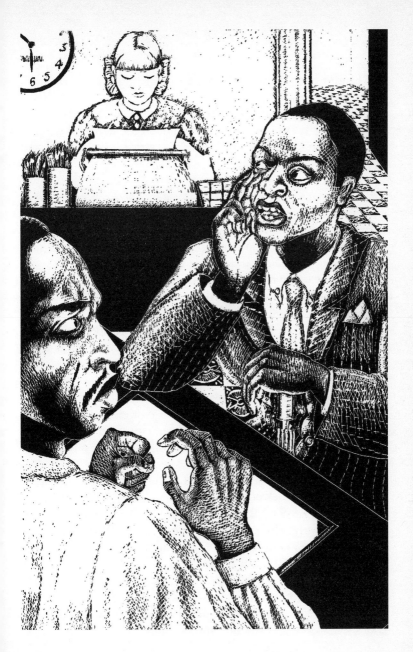

'I want to speak to you like a brother.'

'I am a busy man,' said Obi, again in English. 'If you have nothing else to say . . .'

'I'm sorry to trouble you.'

Mr Mark stood up quickly and went to the door.

For the rest of the morning, Obi felt very happy. He had said no. He had refused a bribe.

Everyone said:

It is not easy to refuse a bribe . . . you may make more trouble by refusing a bribe . . . than by taking it . . . you may make trouble by taking a bribe, and then not doing the thing for which the bribe is given . . . if you refuse a bribe, perhaps a 'brother' or a 'friend' will pretend to be working for you. He will take the bribe and say it is for you . . .

Obi now knew that all these sayings were nonsense. He had refused a bribe. All you had to say was, 'I'm sorry, Mr –. But I can't help you.'

But Obi had to agree that a man could be tempted. Everyone needed money. And Obi was finding it more and more impossible to live on his salary. Each month, he got forty-seven pounds and ten shillings. But he had very little money left at the end of the month.

Every month, he had to pay twenty pounds to the Umuofia Progressive Union and send ten pounds to his parents. And what about the school fees for his young brother, John? Where were they going to come from?

Obi went back to his flat at Ikoyi. After lunch, Obi heard a car stop outside the block of flats.

Obi did not know any of the Europeans who lived in the block of flats. Only one of them spoke to him. An Englishman came to his door once a month to ask for ten shillings. This was to pay for the boy who worked in the garden.

It's a visitor for one of the Europeans, Obi thought.

The car started again. It was a taxi.

There was a quiet knock on Obi's door. Who could it be? Clara was working at the hospital that afternoon.

Perhaps it was Joseph. Joseph was trying to make friends again with Obi. Joseph had told the President of the UPU about Clara. Joseph had thought that the President would speak alone with Obi and stop him marrying this unsuitable woman.

Obi was ready to forget what Joseph had done. But Clara hated Joseph. She never wanted to see him again. She had liked Joseph very much before, but now she hated him with all her heart. Obi was surprised at the hate he saw in Clara.

Obi opened the door. He thought Joseph would be standing there. But he got a surprise. There was a girl standing at the door.

'Good afternoon,' he said with a smile.

'I'm looking for Mr Okonkwo,' she said.

'That's me,' said Obi, again with a smile. 'Come in. Please sit down. I don't think we have met before.'

'No, I'm Elsie Mark.'

'Pleased to meet you, Miss Mark.'

The girl smiled at Obi. She looked very beautiful.

'You must be surprised at my visit,' she said in Ibo.

As soon as she spoke in Ibo, Obi knew why she had come. The smile left his face.

'I'm sorry my brother came to your office this morning. I told him not to.'

Obi did not know what to say. He spoke quickly.

'That's all right,' he said. 'I told your brother that . . . you did very well in your examinations . . . you had a very good Grade One Certificate. Now you must . . . you must do well at the interview with the Board.'

'The most important thing is that I am asked to go for an interview.'

'Yes, I agree,' said Obi.

'But sometimes people with Grade Two or Grade Three are asked to go for an interview but people with Grade One are not asked.'

'Perhaps that happens sometimes,' said Obi. 'But . . . I'm

sorry, would you like a drink . . . would you . . . would you like a Coca-Cola?'

He went to the kitchen, trying to think what to say to this beautiful girl. She took the glass and thanked him.

They sat looking at each other. Suddenly she spoke. 'Last year, three of the girls in our school got Grade One Certificates. But none of them were given a scholarship.'

'Perhaps they did not do well at the interview.'

'No, that wasn't the reason. The reason was that they did not see the members of the Board at home.'

'So you are going to see all the members?'

'Yes.'

'Is a scholarship as important as that?' asked Obi. 'Why doesn't your father or another relation pay for you to go to university?'

'Our father spent all his money on our brother.'

'Was that the man who came to see me today?'

'Yes. He went to England to study medicine, but he failed his exams. He was in England for twelve years. He came back when our father died. He came back without a degree. Now he is a teacher in a secondary school. And we have no more money.

'Please Mr Okonkwo, you must help. I'll do anything you ask.'

Obi liked the girl. She was intelligent. But why was it so important for her to get a university degree? Because a university degree had magic power. It changed a clerk with a salary of one hundred and fifty pounds a year into a Senior Civil Servant with a salary of five hundred and seventy pounds a year – with a car and a flat in the best part of town. What powerful magic!

'I'm sorry . . . very sorry . . . but I . . . I can't make any promises.'

At that moment, a car stopped outside the block of flats and Clara came in. She was surprised when she saw the girl.

'Hello, Clara. This is Miss Mark.'

Clara was not pleased to see this beautiful girl in Obi's flat. The girl stood up.

'I must be going now,' she said.

'I'm sorry, I can't make any promises,' said Obi.

The girl smiled sadly.

'How are you getting back to town?' asked Obi. 'It's not easy to get a taxi from here. I'll take you in my car. Come on, Clara.'

On the drive back to Obi's flat, Clara wanted to know all about the girl. Who was she? What was she doing in Obi's flat? Had Clara come in at the wrong time?'

Obi told Clara she was talking nonsense. He told her about the man who had come to the office in the morning. Then he told her why the girl had come to the flat.

When he had finished speaking, Clara said nothing.

'That's the truth,' said Obi.

'I think you should have listened to the man,' said Clara. 'The man wanted to give you money and you did not listen to him. But the girl wanted to do anything for you and you gave her a drink and drove her back to town. Giving money is not as bad as giving someone your body.'

Obi did not know what to say.

12

Money Troubles

Mr Green once spoke to Obi in a friendly way. It was on the day when he had given Obi the letter to take to the car-dealers. Mr Green had spoken about the insurance[49] on the car.

'Remember,' Mr Green had said, 'you will have to pay

insurance every year. A day will come when you have to find the money to pay the insurance.'

But Obi had forgotten Mr Green's words. He had forgotten about the insurance until the day came one year later. And now the letter was on the table in front of him.

Forty-two pounds! Where was he going to find forty-two pounds? He had only thirteen pounds in the bank. He would have to go to the bank manager and ask for a loan.

No one can say that I have spent my money badly, Obi said to himself. My mother was very ill. She had to go to hospital. I had to send thirty-five pounds home last month. If I had not sent that money home, I could have paid the insurance.

Obi had made friends again with the Union. The President had told him they would wait for the loan to be paid back. But Obi had refused. He had told the President he now had enough money. He did not need to wait to pay back the loan.

The members of UPU had helped Obi to become a Senior Civil Servant. He now had a large salary and he was given a car loan. But he was not given money to pay for the insurance. He was not given money to pay for all the other things that he needed. A Senior Civil Servant cannot live like a poor villager in Umuofia.

Obi got a loan from the bank. He was able to pay the insurance. But there were other things which would soon have to be paid for. He would have to pay for the car licence[50]. He would have to pay for new tyres. The old tyres were dangerous. Four new tyres would cost thirty pounds.

Then there was the electricity bill[51] – another five pounds. Where was the money going to come from?

Obi knew he must save money. He told his servant to spend less money in the market. Every room in the flat had two electric light bulbs. Obi went round the flat and took out one of the bulbs in each room. Then he turned off the water-heater. In future, he would wash in cold water. The servant thought Obi had gone mad!

13

A Quarrel With Clara

Obi was in love with Clara. But they often had quarrels. Obi had studied English Literature. He liked to talk about poetry. But Clara knew nothing about poetry. She liked to go to the cinema. But Obi hated the films they went to see.

Once, Obi had sat beside Clara in the cinema. But he had refused to look at the film. Clara had said it was 'a very good film'. But Obi thought it was terrible.

'I have to sit and listen while you read poetry to me,' said Clara. 'So you must sit with me and watch the films that I like.'

But these quarrels were not very important. They were the quarrels which lovers always have. But Obi and Clara had a bigger quarrel – about Obi's money troubles.

One evening, Obi went to visit Clara. Clara immediately saw that he was worried and unhappy.

'What's wrong?' she asked.

'Nothing is wrong,' replied Obi.

But Clara knew he was not telling the truth. She refused to talk to him and they sat together without talking. At last, he had to tell her about the loan from the bank.

'Why didn't you tell me?' she asked. 'Why didn't you tell me about your money troubles?'

'I have no money troubles,' said Obi.

Clara did not reply. She picked up a magazine and started to read.

'You shouldn't read when you have a visitor,' said Obi.

Clara began to cry.

'Clara,' he said, putting his arm round her shoulders. 'Clara.'

But she did not reply. She turned over the pages in the magazine without looking at them.

'Perhaps I should go,' said Obi.
Clara said nothing.
Obi stood up. 'Goodbye.'
Clara sat turning the pages of the magazine.
'Bye-bye,' she said, without looking at him.

The next morning, a parcel arrived for Obi in his office. It was from Clara.

Obi carefully opened the parcel. What was he going to find? Had Clara sent him back his engagement ring? Was their love at an end?

There was no ring inside the parcel. There were ten five pound notes. And there was a message from Clara.

Darling,
I'm sorry about last night. Go to the bank immediately and pay back the loan. See you tonight.
Love, Clara

Obi's eyes began to fill with tears. Where had Clara got so much money? She got a good salary as a nurse. And she had gone to England on a government scholarship. She did not have to pay back the money. But fifty pounds was a lot of money. How had she got it?

He knew that he could not take the money. He had to give it back to her. But how? He had to find a way. He did not want to quarrel with her again.

Clara was getting ready to go out when Obi arrived. 'We're meeting Sam Okoli and his girlfriend tonight,' she told him.

'We're going to a dance at the Imperial Club. What did the bank manager say when you paid him back the money?'

'I did not go to the bank,' replied Obi. 'How can I take so much money from you? It's not possible.'

'It's only a loan,' said Clara. 'If you don't want it, you can give it back to me.' She held out her hand.

Obi took her hand and pulled her towards him. But he did not give her back the money.

'Thank you for your help,' he said. 'It's very kind of you to want to help me.'

They went to the Imperial Club in Obi's car. He was now able to drive the car and did not have a driver. The car-park at the Imperial was full of cars. At last Obi found a place to park. He was helped by a number of small boys.

'Me look your car for you,' they all shouted together.

'OK,' replied Obi. 'You look him well.'

'Lock your door carefully,' Obi said quietly to Clara.

Obi and Clara met the Hon Sam Okoli and his girlfriend in the Imperial. They drank together and they danced. It was a happy evening. And Obi was pleased that it was not an expensive evening. They did not drink beer or champagne which were very expensive.

At two o'clock in the morning, they left the Imperial. Clara and Obi said goodnight to the Hon Sam Okoli and his girlfriend. They walked back to the car.

Obi unlocked the door on his side and leant over to open the door for Clara. But her door was unlocked.

'Didn't I tell you to lock your door?'

'I did lock it,' she said.

'Oh, no!' cried Obi.

'What's wrong?' asked Clara.

'Your money.'

'Where is it? Where did you leave it?'

Obi pointed at the glove-box[52]. It was empty.

Obi pointed at the glove-box. It was empty.

He quietly got out of the car. He looked around. The car-park was empty. Clara opened her door and got out too. She took his hand in hers and said, 'Let's go.'

Obi was shaking.

'Let's go, Obi,' she said again, and opened the car door for him.

14

Back to Umuofia

After Christmas, Obi got a letter from his father. His mother was ill in hospital again. Obi's father wanted Obi to take local leave and come home.

Local leave was given to all Senior Civil Servants. It had been given at first to Europeans in the Civil Service. But now it was given to Nigerians. Mr Green thought this was wrong.

'The reason for local leave,' he told Obi, 'was to give Europeans a holiday in a cool place away from the heat of Lagos. But you Nigerians don't need local leave.'

Obi said that it was not his business. It was for the government to decide.

When Mr Green had left the office, Obi read his father's letter again. He saw that his father wanted to speak with him about an important matter. Obi knew what the 'important matter' was. His parents had heard about Clara.

Obi had written to them some months ago. He had told them that there was a girl he wanted to marry. But he had not told them she was an *osu*. But now he knew that someone else had told them.

Obi was given leave from 10th to 24th February. He was going to go to Umuofia by car. He was going to leave very early in the morning. He would stay the night in Benin and reach Umuofia the next day.

Clara spent the whole day – and the whole night – in Obi's flat to help him with his packing. When they were in bed, Clara said that she had something to tell Obi. She began to cry.

'What's wrong? What's wrong?' he asked.

At last she spoke.

'Perhaps it's wrong to get married,' she said. 'I have thought about everything carefully. There are two reasons why we should not get married.'

'What are they?' asked Obi.

'Your family will be against our marriage. I don't want to make trouble between you and your family.'

'Nonsense,' said Obi. 'Now tell me, what's the second reason?'

But she refused to tell him what the second reason was. It wasn't important.

'I'll tell you what the other reason is,' he said angrily. 'You don't want to marry a man who cannot pay his insurance.'

He knew that this was not true. She started to cry again. He pulled her towards him and began to kiss her.

'I'm very sorry, darling,' he said.

Obi started his journey at six in the morning. Although he had two weeks' leave, Obi was going to stay only one week in Umuofia. He did not have enough money to stay for two weeks. Everyone in Umuofia knew he had a large salary. They would want him to spend a lot of money.

But Obi had very little money to spend. He had exactly thirty-four pounds. Twenty-five pounds was the local leave allowance which was paid to all Senior Civil Servants. The rest was what was left from his January salary. Thirty-four pounds was enough to spend on two weeks' leave at home. But sixteen pounds, ten shillings had to be paid for his younger brother John's school fees. This did not leave him enough to spend on giving feasts for the villagers.

'Where is Mother?' he asked as soon as he arrived at the house.

'Your mother came back from hospital last week,' said his father. 'She is in her room.'

Obi looked at his mother lying on her bed. She looked very ill. Tears came into his eyes.

'I am much better now,' said his mother. 'You did not see me when I was ill. Now I am much better. How is your work? Are Umuofia people in Lagos well? How is Joseph?'

'They are all well. Yes, very well. Yes, yes.' But his heart was full of sadness as he spoke.

15

'I Shall Kill Myself'

Obi talked with his father when the rest of the family had gone to bed.

'You wrote to me some time ago about a girl,' his father began. 'You said you were thinking of marrying her.'

'This is why I have come,' said Obi. 'I want to talk to you about the marriage. I have not enough money to get married now. But we can talk about it.'

'Do we know this girl? Where does she come from? What is her name?'

'She is a daughter of Okeke, a family in Mbaino.'

'Which Okeke?' asked Obi's father. 'I know three families in

Mbaino of that name. One was a schoolteacher. But I'm sure it is not that one.'

'That is the one,' said Obi.

'Josiah Okeke?'

'That is his name.'

'You cannot marry this girl,' said his father.

'Why?'

'Her family is *osu*.'

'That is not important,' said Obi. 'We are Christians. We do not believe in *osu*. The Bible says that all men are the same. Before they knew Christ, our fathers believed in spirits. An *osu* was a man given to a god. And we did not marry his children or his children's children. But now we are Christians. We do not believe in *osu*.'

There was a long silence.

'I know Josiah Okeke very well,' said Mr Okonkwo. 'He is a good man and a good Christian. But he and his family are *osu*. Our people think *osu* is like a terrible disease[53] – a disease which cannot be cured. Please, my son, do not bring this disease into your family. Who will marry your daughters? Whose daughters will marry your sons? Think of that, my son.'

'But all this will change. In ten years' time *osu* will be forgotten.'

The old man shook his head sadly, but said no more.

Obi did not sleep well that night. But he was not unhappy. His father had asked him not to marry Clara. But he had not said that he *must not* marry Clara.

As soon as he woke up, Obi went to see his mother. It was still dark, but she was awake. She had not slept much because of the pain in her stomach.

'I had a bad dream one night,' she said to Obi. 'I dreamt that I felt something on my skin. I looked down and saw that there were ants all over my body. They had eaten up the bed under me. I did not know the meaning of this strange dream.

'In the morning, your father came in with a letter from Joseph.

In the letter, Joseph told us that you were going to marry an *osu*. I then knew the meaning of my dream. It meant my death.

'I will only say one thing. If you want to marry this girl, then wait until I am dead. You will not have long to wait.'

She stopped speaking. Obi was afraid when he saw the mad look on her face.

'Mother!' he cried.

'If you do marry this girl while I am alive, I will kill myself.'

She fell back on the bed and said nothing more.

Obi went back to his room and stayed there for the rest of the day. Friends and relatives came to the house to see him. But he refused to see anyone. He said that he was sick after the long journey.

That night, his father came into his room. His father asked how he was. Obi said nothing. His father sat beside the bed and said nothing also.

'I shall go back to Lagos the day after tomorrow,' said Obi.

'You said you were going to stay for a week.'

'I think it would be better if I leave earlier.'

16

More Trouble

When he got back to Lagos, Obi went to see Clara. He told Clara about his visit to Umuofia. He told her what his father and mother had said about their marriage.

'Everything will be all right,' he said. 'My mother has not been very well for a long time. All we have to do is wait.'

Clara listened. When he stopped talking, she looked at him. She asked him if he had finished. He did not answer.

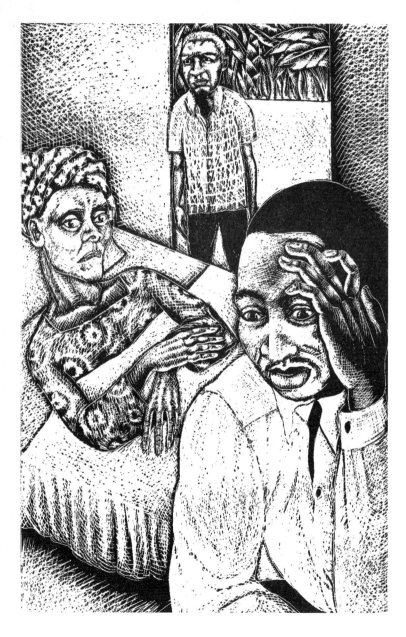

'If you do marry this girl while I am alive, I will kill myself.'

'Have you finished?' she asked again.

'Finished what?'

'Your story.'

Obi said nothing.

'It is not important,' said Clara. 'I should have known from the beginning that it would end this way.'

'What are you talking about?' asked Obi.

She took the engagement ring off her finger and held it out to him.

'What are you doing?' he asked.

'If you don't take it, I will throw it out of the window.'

'If you want.'

Clara did not throw the ring out of the window. She went outside to the car. She opened the door and put the ring in the glove-box.

Clara came back into the room. She went to the window and looked outside.

They sat in silence for a long time. At last, Clara spoke, 'Isn't it time you were going?'

'Yes,' he said, and got up.

'There was something I wanted to tell you,' said Clara. 'But it is not important now. I should have been more careful. I should have taken better care of myself[54].'

Obi was shaking.

'What is it?' he asked. But he knew immediately what was wrong.

The first doctor Obi and Clara went to was an old man. Obi told the doctor what they wanted. At first, the old doctor was ready to help. But then he said he would not help.

'I'm sorry,' he said. 'I can't help you. I could be sent to prison. Why don't you marry the girl? She is very beautiful.'

'I don't want to marry him,' said Clara.

'What wrong with him?' asked the doctor. 'He looks a nice young man to me.'

'I say I don't want to marry him,' she shouted. 'Isn't that enough?'

The next doctor they went to was young and wanted money.

'I shall do it for you if you can pay me,' he said. 'I want thirty pounds.'

Obi asked the doctor if he would do it for less than thirty pounds. But the young doctor said no.

'I'm sorry,' he said. 'It is a small operation, but I could be sent to prison. Go and think about it. If you want the operation done, come back tomorrow at two with the money.'

As they were leaving, the doctor asked Obi: 'Why don't you marry her?' Obi did not reply.

17

Obi is Afraid

Obi now had to find thirty pounds. And it had to be found before two o'clock the next day. There was also the fifty pounds he must give back to Clara.

He counted the money he had brought back from Umuofia. There was twelve pounds and a few coins. He had given only five pounds to his mother and nothing to his father.

Obi did not know what to do. He could go to a money-lender. The money-lender would loan Obi thirty pounds. But Obi would have to sign a paper to say he had been loaned sixty! Obi would have to pay back a loan of sixty pounds. That was impossible. He could never do that.

Obi thought of going to the President of the UPU. But that

was also impossible. The President would want to know why he needed the money. No. He could not go to the UPU for help.

Then Obi remembered the Honourable Sam Okoli. He was a friend of Clara's. Obi was sure he would help. But Obi decided not to tell the Honourable Sam Okoli why he wanted the money.

Obi and Clara arrived at the doctor's house at two o'clock. The doctor counted the money carefully. Then he folded the notes and put them in his pocket.

'Come back at five o'clock,' he told Obi.

But Obi could not drive away. He sat in the car and waited. He was terribly afraid. He was sure that something was going to go wrong.

He saw Clara come out with the doctor. They got into a car. Clara saw Obi in his car, but she quickly turned her eyes away.

Obi wanted to get out of his car and shout: 'Stop. Let's go and get married now.' But he could not and did not. The doctor's car drove away. Obi suddenly made up his mind. He had to stop the operation. He started the car and drove down the street. He tried to follow the doctor's car. But it was too late. The car had gone and he did not know where.

Obi drove through the streets of Lagos all afternoon. He looked everywhere for the doctor's car. At last he stopped. He did not know where he was. The afternoon heat was terrible. It was the hottest time of the year. Obi wanted to die.

At five o'clock, he drove back to the doctor's house. The doctor was not there. Obi waited an hour and a half. At last the doctor came back without Clara.

'Where is she?' asked Obi.

'Don't worry. She'll be all right. But I want her to stay in hospital for the night.'

Next morning, Obi was at the doctor's house early. But there were many people waiting to see the doctor. Obi pushed his way to the front. As soon as the doctor's door opened, he walked in.

'Where is she?' shouted Obi.

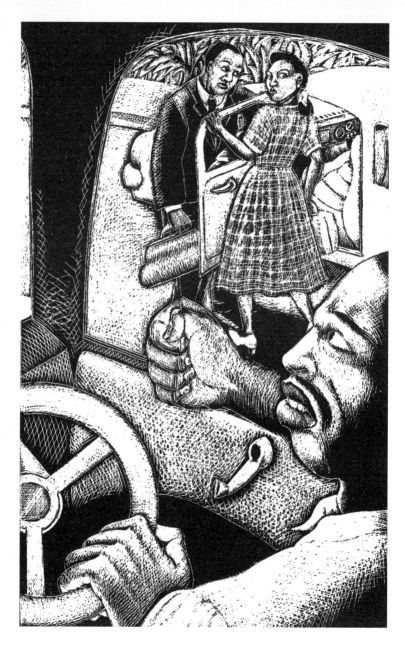

He was terribly afraid. He was sure that something was going to go wrong.

'There's nothing to worry about,' the doctor said. 'There's been a little trouble. That's all. A friend of mine is looking after her in hospital.'

The doctor gave Obi the name of the hospital.

In the hospital, a nurse told Obi that Clara was very ill. Visitors were not allowed to see her.

18

The Death of Mrs Okonkwo

After his leave ended, Obi went back to work. Bad news was waiting for him.

'How much of your leave allowance have you spent?' Mr Omo asked him.

Obi did not understand why Mr Omo wanted to know.

'The twenty-five pounds is for your travel expenses,' said Mr Omo. 'You have to pay back any money you have not spent on travelling.'

Obi looked at a map to find the distance from Lagos to Umuofia. It was not far enough. Obi would have to pay back ten pounds! So he told Mr Omo that he had gone to the Cameroons. He had spent all the money on travelling.

Obi was now in terrible trouble. He made a decision. He would stop paying back the money to the UPU. And he would not tell them. When they asked him why he was not paying the money, he would say that he needed the money to help his family. They would understand that. They all had to help their families.

But more bad news was waiting for him in the office the next day. There was a letter on his desk. Obi had forgotten about income tax[55]. He had to pay tax on his salary every year. Now he had to find thirty-two pounds!

And another letter arrived for him. It was a letter he had sent to Clara in hospital. He looked at it and saw that it had not been opened. Clara had sent it back to him unopened.

Obi had written the letter because she had refused to see him in the hospital. When he had gone to see her, she had turned away from him. After that, she had told the nurses not to let him in again.

Clara was in hospital for seventy days. As soon as she was better, she left Lagos and went home. Obi had wanted to pay her the fifty pounds. But he was not able to do this. He did not have enough money.

Then came more bad news. His mother died. He sent as much money as he could to pay for the funeral[56]. He decided not to go back to Umuofia himself. It was better to send money than spend it on petrol.

But the money Obi sent was not enough. A member of the UPU had been at home when she died. He told everyone that it was shameful. Mrs Okonkwo had given birth to a son who had been educated in England. She should have had a much better funeral. And it was a greater shame that Obi had not gone to Umuofia for the funeral.

Mr Green gave him two days' leave. He went home and locked himself in his flat. He lay on the bed until he heard a knock at the door. It was Joseph.

Joseph arrived with a box of cold beer. People from Umuofia began to arrive. They greeted Obi and said they were sad to hear of his mother's death. Obi sat in a chair and said nothing. The others sat round and talked to one another. Joseph gave them the cold beer. At last, they all went and Obi was left alone.

For some days, Obi felt a terrible sadness. He thought about his mother. He remembered her when he was a young boy. He remembered how she had taken care of him. The days passed and the sadness went away. Obi was back at work and he had other things to think about.

19

'Why Did He Do It?'

It was the time for scholarships once again. There was a lot of work to do.

One afternoon, Obi was getting ready to do some work at home. A large car stopped outside the block of flats. A Nigerian got out of the car. He looked like a very rich businessman. Who could it be?

The man knocked at Obi's door. Obi went to open it.

'Good afternoon,' said Obi.

'Good afternoon,' said the man. 'Are you Mr Okonkwo?'

Obi said yes and invited the man in. 'Please sit down.'

'My son is going to England in September,' said the man. 'I want him to get a scholarship. Here is fifty pounds, if you can help me.'

Obi told the man that it was not possible.

'I do not give the scholarships,' said Obi. 'My job is to make a list of the best students. These students will then go for an interview before the Scholarship Board.'

'Make sure my son's name is on that list,' said the man. 'That's all you have to do.'

Obi remembered the boy's name. He had good results in the exam. His name was sure to be on the list.

'Why don't you pay for him?' asked Obi. 'You have money. The scholarship is for poor people.'

The man laughed. 'No man in this world has enough money.'

He stood up and put some five pound notes on Obi's table. 'This is a small gift,' he said. 'We will be friends and I will see you again. Don't forget his name.'

The money lay on the table all day and all night. Obi put a newspaper on top of the money.

This is terrible! he said to himself. Terrible!

He woke up in the middle of the night. He lay in bed, thinking. He did not go to sleep again for a long time afterwards.

———

'You dance very well,' Obi told the young girl. He held her in his arms and kissed her on the lips. They forgot about the music and the dancing. They went into Obi's bedroom.

She had done well in the exams. She was sure to be asked to go for an interview before the Scholarship Board. But it was shameful. Obi knew that. He drove her back to town in his car.

———

Other people came. Sometimes it was the students themselves. Sometimes it was their fathers. One man told another: 'The Secretary to the Board takes money, but he always does what he promises.'

There was one thing which Obi would not do. He would not help anyone who did not have good results in the exams.

Time passed and he was able to pay back all the loans. Obi should have been happier. But he was not. He was very unhappy.

Then one day he had a visitor. The man brought twenty pounds. Obi knew that he could not go on.

Obi sat and looked at the money on the table. He did not want to look at it. But he was not able to turn his eyes away.

There was a knock at the door. Obi picked up the money and ran to the bedroom. There was another knock at the door. Obi pushed the notes into his pocket and went to the door.

Obi opened the door. Two men came in. One was his visitor and the other was a stranger.

'Are you Mr Obi Okonkwo?' the stranger asked. Obi said yes, in a quiet voice. The room began to go round and round. The stranger was saying something. But Obi could not understand what he was saying. They searched Obi and found the notes in his pocket. A small mark had been made on each of the notes. Obi had to agree that he had taken them.

The stranger went on talking about bribery and corruption. The other man phoned the police and asked them to send a police car.

Epilogue

*T*he Judge, Mr Green, the man from the British Council, the President of the Umuofia Progressive Union – none of them understood why Obi Okonkwo had taken the bribe.

Now we have read the story of Obi Okonkwo, do we understand why?

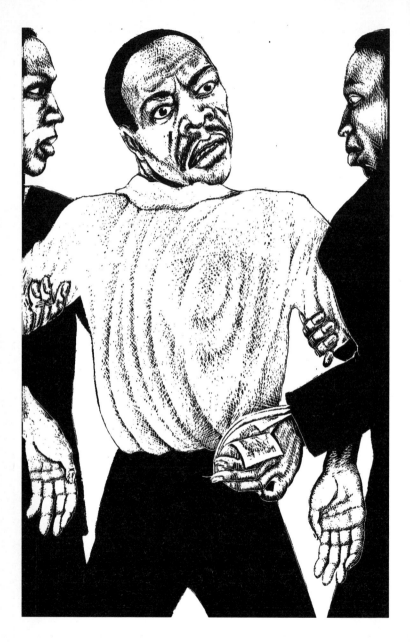

They searched Obi and found the notes in his pocket.

POINTS
FOR
UNDERSTANDING

Points for Understanding

Prologue

1. Obi Okonkwo was found guilty of a crime. What was the crime?
2. What words of the Judge made Obi want to cry?
3. Obi had lost everything.
    (a) What had happened to Obi's mother?
    (b) What had happened to the woman Obi loved?
4. Mr Green said he knew why Obi took the bribe. What did he say was the reason?
5. What was the UPU? Who were members of the UPU?
6. Every member of the UPU paid part of his salary to a fund.
    (a) What was the fund for?
    (b) How had the fund helped Obi Okonkwo?
7. One member of the UPU did not want to give any more help to Obi Okonkwo. What two things had Obi done which made this member angry?

1

1. Why was Obi chosen to go and study in England?
2. When would Obi have to pay back the loan to the UPU?
3. What did Obi's parents do a few days before Obi left Umuofia?
4. What did Mr Ikedi say that Obi must not do?
5. What kind of presents did the people of Umuofia give to Obi?

2

1. Who was Joseph Okeke? What was his work?
2. Why did Joseph say it was important to learn to dance?
3. Why did Obi go out for a walk by himself?

3

1. How did Obi's stay in England change him?
2. Where had Obi met Clara before?
3. What did Obi think of Clara when he first saw her?

4   Obi spoke to Clara in the lounge. Was Clara pleased to meet him again?
5   Clara came to Obi's cabin and gave him some tablets. What were the tablets for?
6   Obi did not sleep that night. What could he not decide?
7   How did Obi make friends with John Macmillan?
8   Obi and John Macmillan went for a walk in Funchal. Who came with them?
9   What happened when Obi and Clara were left alone on the deck of the boat?

4

1   Obi gave a talk in the Nigerian Students' Union in London. What did he talk about?
2   'I do it, but you no get government receipt.'
    (a) What was the young customs officer going to do with the money Obi gave him?
    (b) Explain why the young man speaks in this way.
3   Why did the Secretary of the UPU think they should have a talk with the men on the Interview Board?
4   Why did the President think it was not necessary?
5   Did the Secretary agree with the President?

5

1   Obi asked Clara to marry him. Did she agree?
2   What did Clara ask Obi not to do?
3   What did Obi think when he saw Clara sitting in the back seat of the Honourable Sam Okoli's car?

6

1   What did Obi and the Chairman of the Interview Board talk about?
2   'I don't know how to answer your question,' Obi said to a member of the Interview Board.
    (a) What was the question?
    (b) Why did Obi say it was a foolish question?
3   'The law says that no one must pay bride-price,' Obi said to Joseph.
    (a) What was bride-price?
    (b) Had the law stopped people paying bride-price?

7

1 How did Obi travel to Umuofia?
2 Why did the policeman not take the bribe offered by the driver's mate?
3 Why did the lorry stop about a quarter of a mile along the road?
4 Why was the lorry driver angry with Obi?
5 Obi could not understand why Clara wanted their love to be secret. Was Clara's friendship with the Hon Sam Okoli the reason?

8

1 Describe Obi's welcome back to Umuofia.
2 Why did Mr Okonkwo not give any gifts to the rainmaker?
3 Why was Obi sad when he saw his mother?
4 The church gave Mr Okonkwo two pounds a month.
    (a) Why did the church give Mr Okonkwo the money?
    (b) Why was most of the money given back to the church?

9

1 What job was Obi given in the Civil Service?
2 Why was Obi sent first to Mr Omo's office?
3 'This is a wonderful day,' Obi told Clara on the phone.
    (a) What was going to happen at two o'clock?
    (b) Why did Obi have sixty pounds in his pocket?
    (c) Where were Obi and Clara going to go?
4 Obi was given a government flat.
    (a) Where was the flat?
    (b) Why was the flat special?
5 What did Clara say was the reason she and Obi could not get married?
6 'Nonsense!' Obi shouted loudly. Why did Obi shout this word loudly?
7 What did Joseph say when Obi said that he was going to marry Clara?
8 It was shameful that people still believed in such a thing.
    (a) Explain what an *osu* was.
    (b) Why did Obi think it was shameful that people still believed in *osu*?
9 How much did Obi pay for the engagement ring?

10 Obi told Joseph about his engagement.
    (a) Was Joseph pleased?
    (b) Who did Joseph say would not agree to the marriage?
    (c) Who did Joseph say would not be pleased if Obi married an *osu*?

10

1 Why was 1st December 1956 an important date in Obi's life?
2 'He go make plenty money there,' said the clerk.
    (a) Why did the clerk think Obi would make plenty of money?
    (b) What was Joseph's reply?
3 Describe the arrival of Obi and Joseph at the meeting.
4 Obi had a request to make to the UPU.
    (a) What was the request?
    (b) Did the members of the UPU agree to Obi's request?
5 'I want to speak to you like a father,' the President of the UPU said to Obi.
    (a) What did the President say to Obi?
    (b) What did Obi do?
    (c) When did Obi say he would pay back the loan?

11

1 Mr Mark came to see Obi in his office.
    (a) Why was Mr Mark surprised when he saw Miss Tomlinson?
    (b) What language did Mr Mark speak in?
    (c) What did Mr Mark want?
2 Why did everyone say it was not easy to refuse a bribe?
3 How had Obi refused Mr Mark's bribe?
4 There was a quiet knock on Obi's door.
    (a) Who did Obi think was at the door?
    (b) Why was Obi surprised?
5 Why had Miss Mark come to see Obi?
6 What did Obi do when Clara arrived suddenly?
7 'I think you should have listened to the man,' said Clara. Why did Clara think Obi should have listened to the man?

12

1   But Obi had forgotten Mr Green's words.
     (a) What had Mr Green told Obi?
     (b) What was on the table in front of Obi?
2   Why would Obi have to go and see the bank manager?
3   Why could Obi not live like a poor villager in Umuofia?
4   What other things would Obi soon have to pay for?

13

1   Clara sent Obi a parcel. What was in the parcel?
2   What happened when Obi tried to give the money back to Clara?
3   At last Obi found a place to park.
     (a) Where were they going to spend the evening?
     (b) What did Obi say to Clara before they left the car?
4   At two o'clock in the morning, Obi and Clara walked back to the
     car. What did they find?

14

1   Why did Obi's father ask him to come home?
2   What was the important matter Obi's father wanted to talk to
     Obi about?
3   'There are two reasons why we should not get married,' Clara said
     to Obi. What were the reasons Clara gave?
4   Why was Obi going to stay only one week in Umuofia?
5   Why was Obi's heart full of sadness when he saw his mother?

15

1   'We are Christians,' said Obi. Why should Christians not believe
     in *osu*?
2   Why did his father think Obi should not marry an *osu*?
3   'I had a bad dream one night,' said Obi's mother.
     (a) What was the dream?
     (b) What did Obi's mother say was the meaning of the dream?
4   What did Obi's mother say she would do if Obi married an *osu*?
5   When did Obi decide to go back to Lagos?

16

1 'Everything will be all right,' Obi told Clara.
   (a) Did Clara believe him?
   (b) What did Clara do with the engagement ring?
2 'There was something I wanted to tell you,' said Clara. What had happened to Clara?
3 Why was the old doctor not ready to help them?
4 The old doctor asked Obi why he did not marry Clara. What did Clara shout when she heard this?
5 Why was the young doctor ready to help?
6 How much was the operation going to cost?

17

1 Why could Obi not go to a money-lender?
2 Why could Obi not go to the President of the UPU?
3 Who did Obi borrow the money from?
4 Obi saw Clara and the doctor get into a car.
   (a) What did Obi want to do?
   (b) What did Obi do all afternoon?
5 Where did Clara go?
6 Why was Obi not able to see her?

18

1 Why did Mr Omo want to know how far Obi had travelled?
2 What decision did Obi make?
3 What bad news was in the letter waiting for Obi on his desk?
4 Why was Obi not able to visit Clara in hospital?
5 How long was Clara in hospital? What did she do when she came out of hospital?
6 Why could Obi not pay Clara back the fifty pounds?
7 A member of the UPU had been in Umuofia for Obi's mother's funeral. What two things did he say were shameful about the funeral?

19

1   A rich Nigerian businessman came to see Obi. What did the man want?
2   What did the man leave on Obi's table?
3   Why was Obi not able to sleep?
4   What was the one thing which Obi would not do?
5   One day Obi had a visitor.
     (a) How much money did he bring?
     (b) Where did he leave the money?
6   Where did Obi hide the money when he heard another knock at the door?
7   Two men came into Obi's flat. Who were the two men and why had they come?

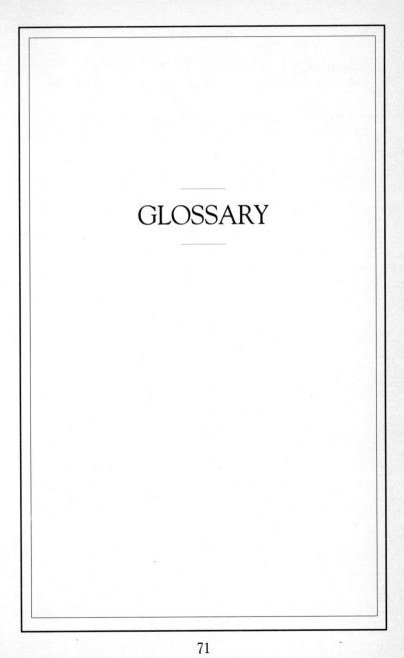

GLOSSARY

Glossary

1 **trial** (page 5)

when the police think someone has committed a crime, they arrest him/her. Then a trial is held to decide whether the accused person did commit the crime or not. The trial is held in a courtroom. A Judge is in charge of the trial. If the court decides that the accused person did commit the crime, he/she is found guilty. The Judge then decides the punishment. For example, the Judge can send the person to prison. A trial is also called a court-case.

2 **Civil Servant** – *Senior Civil Servant* (page 5)

Civil Servants are officials who work in government offices. A Senior Civil Servant is an official in the Civil Service who has an important job and makes important decisions.

3 **bribe** – *take a bribe* (page 5)

to bribe someone is to give them money to do something wrong. An official who takes a bribe helps the person who gives him/her the money.

4 **promise** – *a young man of great promise* (page 5)

a young man of great promise is a young man who does well at school and at university. Everyone thinks that he will later become an important person in his country.

5 **Club** – *Officials' Club* (page 5)

an officials' club is a place where Senior Civil Servants and other important people can meet. There is usually a bar and a restaurant in an officials' club.

6 **boss** (page 5)

the chief person in an office or any place where people work.

7 **Union** – *Umuofia Progressive Union* (page 7)

a Union is a number of people who join together in order to help one another. The members of the Umuofia Progressive Union – the UPU – all come from Umuofia, a small town in Eastern Nigeria. The President and the Secretary are important officials in the Union.

8 **salary** (page 7)

the money paid each month to an official for doing his work.

9 **discuss** (page 7)

to talk about something important.

10 **law** – *to study law* (page 7)
    a lawyer is a person who is trained to work in a courtroom. Before
    a person can become a lawyer, they have to study law at a
    university. A person who is accused of a crime needs the help of a
    lawyer at their trial.
11 **woman** – *get involved with an unsuitable woman* (page 7)
    in some parts of the world, a man is not allowed to marry a
    woman unless his family and the other people in his town agree.
    The members of the UPU have heard that Obi has made friends
    with a woman and they do not think he should marry her.
12 **shameful** (page 8)
    to do something shameful is to do something which people think
    is very wrong.
13 **distinction** (page 9)
    to pass an exam with distinction is to pass the exam with very
    high marks.
14 **scholarship** (page 9)
    money given to students to help them continue their studies at
    college or university. A scholarship is a gift and the student does
    not have to pay the money back.
15 **loan** (page 9)
    money given to a person who says he will pay the money back later.
16 **wine** – *palm wine* (page 9)
    an alcoholic drink made from liquid which comes from the palm tree.
17 **minister** (page 9)
    a person who preaches in a church.
18 **temptations** (page 9)
    Mr Ikedi is saying that Obi was be able to do things in England
    which are not allowed in his own country. To tempt someone is
    to encourage them to do something which is wrong.
19 **clerk** (page 10)
    a clerk works in an office. Clerks type letters and keep letters and
    other papers in files (see Glossary no. 42).
20 **sinful** (page 11)
    to do something sinful is to do something which is against the
    laws of God.
21 **proud** – *to feel proud of* (page 11)
    to feel proud of your country is to believe that your country is a
    good country.

22 **cabin** (page 11)
   a small room on a boat like a bedroom in a hotel. The passengers
   sleep in their cabins. They sit and talk to one another in the
   lounge.

23 **deck** (page 12)
   the open part of a boat where the passengers can walk around and
   look out over the sea.

24 **calm** (page 12)
   when there is no wind, the sea is calm. When the sea is calm, it is
   flat and smooth. A boat sails smoothly on a calm sea. When the
   wind becomes strong, the sea becomes rough. Passengers on a
   boat often feel very sick when the sea is rough.

25 **Ibo** (page 12)
   the language of the Ibo people who live in Eastern Nigeria.

26 **tablets** (page 12)
   small pills which a person swallows when they feel ill.

27 **make up one's mind** (page 13)
   to make up your mind is to make a decision. Obi was not able to
   decide whether Clara wanted to be friends with him or not.

28 **corruption** (page 16)
   a corrupt person is a person who takes bribes.

29 **customs officer** (page 16)
   when you come into a country, you have to go through customs.
   The customs official tells you how much money – customs duty –
   you have to pay on the goods you are bringing into the country.

30 **radiogram** (page 16)
   you can use a radiogram either to listen to the radio or to play
   records.

31 **receipt** – '*I do it, but you no get government receipt*' (page 16)
   a receipt is a piece of paper saying that you have paid the customs
   duty. Obi knows that the young customs officer is corrupt. If the
   customs officer does not write a receipt, he can keep the money
   for himself. The young man is not well educated and does not
   speak grammatical English. In grammatical English, this sentence
   would be: 'I can do it (make the duty less), but you will not get a
   government receipt.' There are some other examples of
   ungrammatical English in this story.

32 **praised** (page 17)
   to praise something or someone is to say that they are very good.

33 **interview** (page 17)

at an interview for a job, you are asked many questions about yourself and about why you want the job. The people who ask the questions are the Interview Board. If you do well at the interview, you are given the job. The person in charge of the Interview Board is called the Chairman.

34 **ring** – *buy her a ring* (page 17)

when a man and a woman agree to get married, they become engaged. The man gives the woman a ring which is called an engagement ring.

35 **pretended** (page 18)

to pretend to do something is to do something which is not true.

36 **superiors** – *respectful to your superiors* (page 19)

Joseph believes that you must always be polite when speaking to your superiors – people who are more important than you are.

37 **bride-price** (page 19)

money paid by a man to the family of the woman he wants to marry.

38 **mate** – *driver's mate* (page 20)

a mate is a man who works with another man and helps him in his job.

39 **rainmaker** (page 23)

some of the people in Umuofia are not Christians. They believe that there are many gods or spirits everywhere around them – in the trees and in the stones. A rainmaker is a man who is able to speak to the spirits. He gives the spirits gifts or presents which are called sacrifices. If the spirits are pleased with the sacrifices, they do what the rainmaker asks them to do.

40 **kola nut** (page 23)

a nut from the kola tree. Kola nuts are often broken as a sacrifice to the spirits. The soft inside of the nut is chewed by people who meet together. Isaac Okonkwo is a Christian and he does not believe in spirits. So he does not want a kola nut to be broken in his house as a sacrifice to the spirits.

41 **quarrel** (page 24)

when people do not agree with each other, they sometimes have an argument or a quarrel.

42 **file** – *local leave file* (page 26)

local leave is a short holiday given to Civil Servants. All the letters and papers to do with local leave are kept together in a file – a cover for holding letters and papers.

43 **allowance** – *clothing allowance* (page 26)
money given to a Senior Civil Servant so that he can buy the
clothes which he needs for his job.

44 **osu** (page 27)
when Christianity was brought to Nigeria by the British, many
Nigerians became Christians. But they did not forget all their old
beliefs. Many believed in *osu*. *Osu* were people who, many years
ago, had been made servants of a spirit or a god. Their children
and their grandchildren also became *osu*. People in Nigeria who
were not *osu* never married an *osu*.

45 **custom** (page 29)
the custom is the way things have always been done in the past.
When a man wanted to get married, it was the custom for him to
tell his mother and father. The man's family then went to meet
the woman's family before the marriage was agreed.

46 **request** (page 32)
to make a request is to ask for something.

47 **spy** (page 35)
someone who watches another person and listens to what they
say.

48 **apply for** (page 36)
to apply for a scholarship is to ask to be given a scholarship.
When you apply, you have to fill in an application form. You
write your name, your school, the examinations you have passed,
etc. on the application form.

49 **insurance** (page 41)
when you own a car, you have to pay money every year to an
insurance company. If you have an accident, the insurance
company pays money for any damage you have done.

50 **licence** – *car licence* (page 42)
when you own a car, you have to pay money to the government
every year for a car licence. The car licence allows you to drive
your car on all roads.

51 **bill** – *electricity bill* (page 42)
a piece of paper from the electricity company which tells you how
much money you have to pay.

52 **glove-box** (page 45)
a small drawer inside a car at the front.

53 *disease* (page 50)
a bad illness or sickness. A doctor can cure a person who has a disease and make him better. But Mr Okonkwo says that *osu* is like a disease that cannot be cured.

54 *myself* – '*I should have taken better care of myself.*' (page 53)
Clara is pregnant – she is going to have a baby. If she had taken care, she would not have become pregnant.

55 *tax* – *income tax* (page 57)
tax is money paid to the government. Your income is the same as your salary – the money you are paid for doing your job. Income tax is a part of your income which you have to pay to the government every year.

56 *funeral* (page 58)
a funeral takes place when a person dies. After the dead body is put into the ground, the family of the dead person invite neighbours and friends to come for a meal.

Shane *by Jack Schaefer*
Old Mali and the Boy *by D. R. Sherman*
Bristol Murder *by Philip Prowse*
Tales of Goha *by Leslie Caplan*
The Smuggler *by Piers Plowright*
The Pearl *by John Steinbeck*
Things Fall Apart *by Chinua Achebe*
The Woman Who Disappeared *by Philip Prowse*
The Moon is Down *by John Steinbeck*
A Town Like Alice *by Nevil Shute*
The Queen of Death *by John Milne*
Walkabout *by James Vance Marshall*
Meet Me in Istanbul *by Richard Chisholm*
The Great Gatsby *by F. Scott Fitzgerald*
The Space Invaders *by Geoffrey Matthews*
My Cousin Rachel *by Daphne du Maurier*
I'm the King of the Castle *by Susan Hill*
Dracula *by Bram Stoker*
The Sign of Four *by Sir Arthur Conan Doyle*
The Speckled Band and Other Stories by *Sir Arthur Conan Doyle*
The Eye of the Tiger *by Wilbur Smith*
The Queen of Spades and Other Stories *by Aleksandr Pushkin*
The Diamond Hunters *by Wilbur Smith*
When Rain Clouds Gather *by Bessie Head*
Banker *by Dick Francis*
No Longer at Ease *by Chinua Achebe*
The Franchise Affair *by Josephine Tey*
The Case of the Lonely Lady *by John Milne*

For further information on the full selection of
Readers at all five levels in the series, please refer
to the Heinemann ELT Readers catalogue.

79

Macmillan Heinemann English Language Teaching
Between Towns Road, Oxford OX4 3PP
A division of Macmillan Publishers Limited
Companies and representatives throughout the world

ISBN 0 435 27225 X

Heinemann is a registered trade mark of Reed Educational and Professional Publishing Ltd

Illustrated by Matilda Harrison
Typography by Adrian Hodgkins
Cover by Matilda Harrison and Threefold Design
Typeset in 11/12.5 pt Goudy
by Joshua Associates Ltd, Oxford
Printed and bound in Spain by Mateu Cromo, S. A.

2004 2003 2002 2001 2000
18 17 16 15 14 13 12 11 10 9